D0516869

This
PJ BOOK
belongs to

_____

_____

PJ Library®

JEWISH BEDTIME STORIES and SONGS

For my father, Alan Kohuth, a great storyteller,
and for my mother, Leslie Kohuth, who supplied my book habit
and showed me how to be a reader and an artist. And for my sister, Emily Kohuth,
who was a child like no other and is now a real mensch.
—J.K.

To muses Pia and Franziska
—R.L.

Visit us on the Web! www.randomhouse.com/kids

Educators and librarians, for a variety of teaching tools, visit us at www.randomhouse.com/teachers

ISBN: 978-0-375-86503-9

MANUFACTURED IN CHINA

10 9 8 7 6 5 4 3 2

First Edition

Estie the Mensch

by Jane Kohuth · illustrated by Rosanne Litzinger

RANDOM HOUSE   NEW YORK

Estie did not always like people.

People hogged the best toys at school.

People pushed on the train.

People wore smelly perfume and asked
her questions she didn't know the answers to.

"And what do you want to be when you grow up, young lady?" asked the neighbor, Mrs. Zipper.

Estie pulled the collar of her jacket over her head. "Turtle," she mumbled.

"Be polite to Mrs. Zipper," said her mother.

But Estie did not like to be polite.

Estie's best friend was her dog, Flopper.

At dinner, Estie crawled under the table with Flopper. Flopper sniffed the family's feet. Estie sniffed the family's feet. Flopper barked when a truck went by. Estie barked when a car went by. Flopper pawed Estie's father's leg. Estie pawed her grandma's leg.

"*Oy, Estie,*" said her grandma. "*Zai a mensch.*"

"That means *be a person,* Es," explained her father.

"A well-behaved person," her mother added.

"A good person," her grandma finished.

But Estie did not want to be a person. Today she wanted to be a dog. She laid her head in her grandma's lap. Her grandma sighed and petted her hair.

Sometimes Estie was a dog.

Other times, she was a turtle.

One day, at the library, Estie was an elephant.

She clomped and stomped and swung her trunk.

"Be a mensch, Estie!" whispered her mother.

At the beach, Estie was a seagull.

She followed the birds. She flapped her wings.

She pecked at the sand and found a nice clamshell.

"Feh. Spit that out, Estie," said her grandma.

"Be a mensch, Estie," her father reminded her.

At the grocery store, Estie was a chimp.

"Oh, Estie. Save it for the monkey bars," her mother sighed.

Estie's parents had a barbecue in the backyard.

"Bzzzzzzzzzzzzz." Estie the fly zoomed around the hamburgers and macaroni salad. Her feelers landed on a cupcake.

"Buzz off, kiddo," said Estie's father. "Dinner first."

Estie licked frosting off her fingers. Her father raised his eyebrows.

"Be a mensch and use a napkin, Es."

On swimming day, Estie was an octopus. She wriggled and stuck her suction-cup hands to the side of the pool.

"Come jump off the diving board, Es!" called her father.

"Why don't you swim a little?" suggested her mother.

Estie shook her tentacles to say no.

"Use your words," said Estie's mother.

"Yeah, be a mensch!" called her father.

When her grandma babysat, Estie was a tiger.

Estie pounced!

"Estie!" gasped Grandma. "You gave me such a fright! Anyone would think you were a jungle cat instead of a beautiful little girl. Come sit in Grandma's lap."

"Grrrr," said Estie. But she rubbed her cheek against her grandma's woolly sweater.

"Purr," said Estie.

"Oy," sighed Grandma.

The next time she spent the day with Estie,
Grandma had a surprise planned.

"Shall we go to the zoo?" she asked.

Estie nodded. Then she and Flopper bounded
around the room, wagging their tails with joy.

At the entrance to the zoo, they met Grandma's friend Violet and
Violet's grandson, Petie.

Grandma introduced Estie and Petie. Estie looked at the ground
and stayed very close to Grandma. But Petie didn't seem to notice.

"Hi, I'm Petie," he said. "I have a pet newt, and I collected twelve worms in the yard yesterday. My big brother's name is Aaron, and he has a new blue bike he got for his birthday. On my birthday, I'm gonna get a racetrack set and an ant farm from Grandma Violet."

Then Petie pulled a worm out of his pocket and handed it to Estie, who nodded and took it carefully, then gave it to Grandma to hold for her.

Petie walked beside Estie. He kept talking. Estie thought she should say something back, but she didn't know what. So as they passed the ostriches, she stretched out her neck and bobbed her head up and down. She ran, picking her knees up high and shaking her fluffy wing feathers.

To Estie's surprise, Petie laughed! His cheeks turned pink and his freckles stood out on his nose. Estie liked this so much that when they passed the flamingos, she balanced on one leg until she started to wobble. Petie laughed again!

When they went into the reptile house, Estie slithered around Petie like a snake and hissed. Petie giggled.

When they passed the alligator pond, Estie snapped her huge jaws and pretended to chomp on something crunchy and delicious. Petie laughed so hard he had to sit down to catch his breath.

And when they stopped to admire the bears,

Estie let out a huge roar.

"You are so fun to talk to!" said Petie.

At the snack stand, their grandmas bought them ice cream cones.
Petie was so excited to get his that he shouted and jumped in the air.

Shlop! His two scoops of vanilla with rainbow sprinkles landed on
the ground. Some monkeys behind them whooped and chattered. To
make Petie feel better, Estie whooped and chattered, too.

But this time, Petie didn't laugh. He started to cry!
The grandmas tried to comfort him.

Estie thought fast. "Wait!" she cried. She grabbed a plastic spoon and shoveled one of her chocolate scoops with chocolate sprinkles onto Petie's empty cone.

"Thanks, Estie!" he said, and stopped crying right away.

"What a generous thing to do," said Violet.

"Well, that's my Estie," said her grandma. "She's a real mensch."

As they left the zoo, Estie thought that it
wasn't so bad being a mensch.
But could you be a mensch *and* a moose?

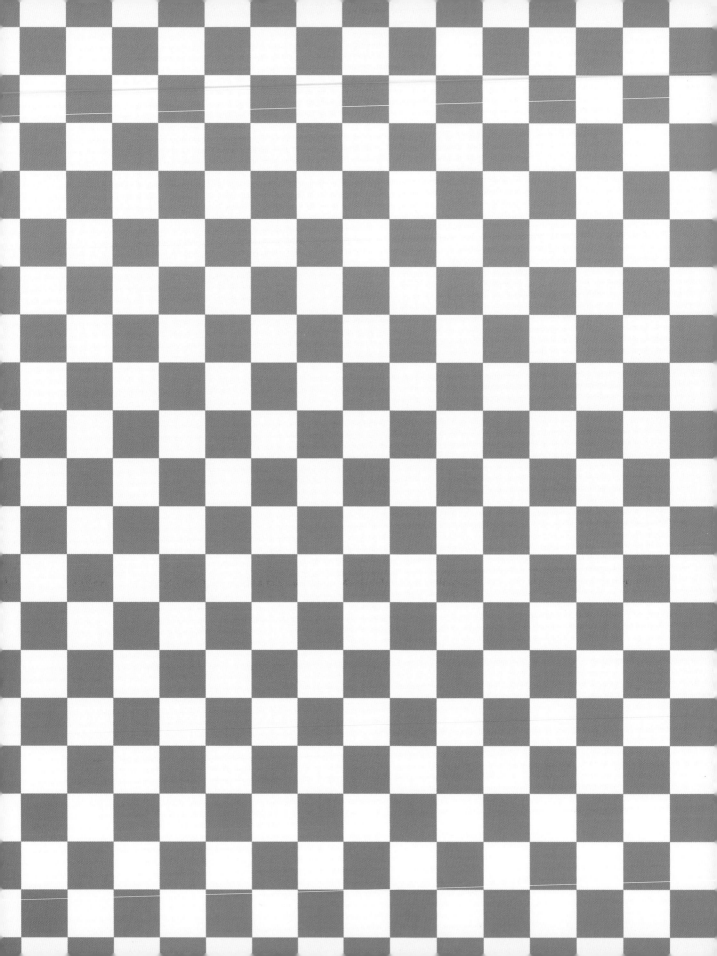